Suzie the Explorer

Written by
Amanda Vraja

Illustrated by
Iesha Wright

For Josie-

"Yunny, you will move mountains!"
Love, Auntie Amanda

One gloomy spring day on Bloomfield Lane,
Suzie was sitting out in the rain.

"Please stop storming," she said in dismay,
"I want to go on an adventure today!"

An hour later, the storm had blown past,
so Suzie prepared for her trip very fast.
She packed up her suitcase, her teddy in hand;
everything was going perfectly as planned.

Then she decided to make a plane,
one that could soar above Bloomfield Lane.
She searched for supplies all around inside
so she could begin her journey worldwide.

5

Suzie made her plane out of boxes and glue,
but her only hope was that it flew.

She grabbed her belongings,
preparing to fly,

gave Mommy a kiss
and waved goodbye.

7

All of a sudden, the plane took off!
But flying above the neighborhood was not enough.
"I want to travel the world!" Suzie yelled,
and with that, the cardboard plane propelled.

8

9

Within one day of her adventurous flight,
Suzie had seen many beautiful sights.
She had flown to the top of the tallest mountain
and soared over the jungle again and again.

11

She visited the pyramids, danced with the mummies;
ate with the sumo wrestlers, filling their tummies.

Suzie was having so much fun
traveling the world and meeting everyone.

Suddenly, the plane slowed to a dangerous crawl,
and Suzie knew the plane was going to stall.

She tried not to crash, for that would not be good,
but it was too late.. and she crashed into the woods!

"Where am I? What should I do?"
exclaimed little Suzie, not having a clue.
She grabbed her teddy and hugged him so,
she was scared, not knowing where to go.

Suzie searched through the forest she was in,
but had no idea where to begin.
Then, she decided to walk toward the sun,
hoping she would find someone.

She came across a shallow stream,
where she decided to rest and began to daydream.
Thinking of ways to leave this land,
suddenly, Suzie thought of a plan!

"I've got it!" she yelled, as she wrote down her plan,
"I can make another plane, and I know that I can!"

She gathered up leaves and branches galore
until her little hands couldn't carry anymore.

Her makeshift plane was smaller than the last,
but she needed it to work, and she needed it fast.
She piled her belongings in the back of the plane,
hoping it would fly her home to Bloomfield Lane.

Much to her surprise, the little plane started!
Smiling with joy, little Suzie departed.

Back in the sky, she remembered her way
and knew she would get home that day.

She traveled quickly, though only a beginner,
for she knew she could not be late for dinner.
Mommy was cooking her favorite food,
and being late would not be good.

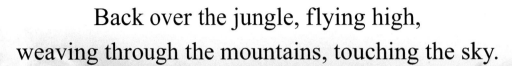

Back over the jungle, flying high,
weaving through the mountains, touching the sky.

Making great timing, she spotted her house.
From the sky, it looked as tiny as a mouse.

At quarter to five, Suzie landed the plane
safely back home to Bloomfield Lane.

She ran inside, for dinner was ready,
and feasted on buttered bread and spaghetti. **29**

Done with dinner, Suzie ran outside,
staring at her plane, remembering the ride.
Then with a grin on her face, she excitedly said,
"I want to go on an adventure again!"

The End

About the Author

Amanda Vraja is thrilled to share Suzie's worldly journey with you and even more excited to see where else she will decide to explore! Amanda lives as a nurse by day, shower singer by night, and has a knack for creative writing. She enjoys staying active, appreciates the lazy days, and laughs at her own jokes. She happily resides in Cleveland, Ohio.

Made in the USA
Middletown, DE
02 July 2021

43528810R00020